THE TWELVE DANCING PRINCESSES

WRITTEN BY

THE BROTHERS GRIMM

ILLUSTRATED BY

RACHEL ISADORA

G. P. PUTNAM'S SONS

There was once a king who had
twelve beautiful daughters.

They slept each night in a locked room, but every morning their shoes
were worn through as if they had danced all night.

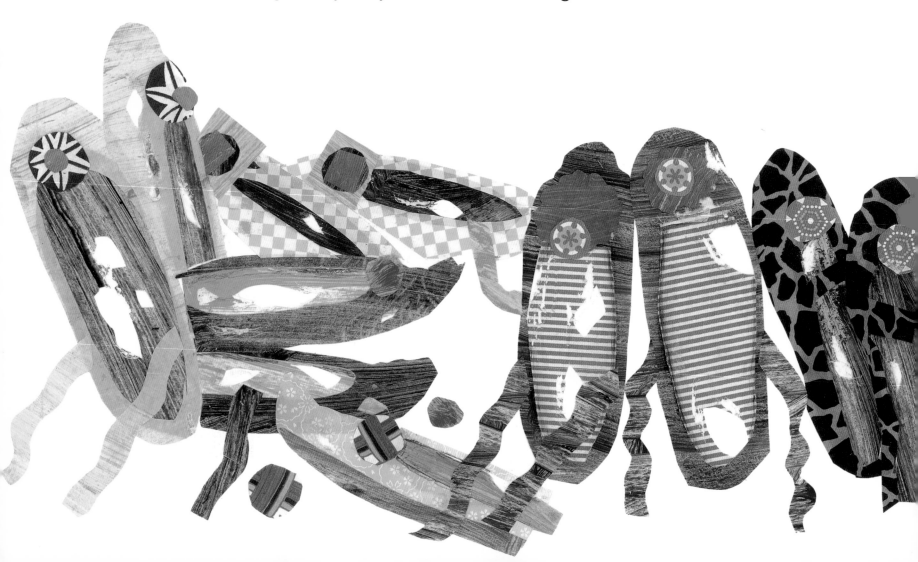

The king made it known that whoever discovered where the princesses went at night could choose a princess for his wife. If after three tries they failed, they would lose their life. Many tried and failed.

One day, a soldier traveling on a road met an old woman. She asked where he was headed and he told her that he was going to try and discover the secret of the princesses.

"That is not difficult," she said. "But you must not drink the wine brought to you, and you must pretend to be asleep."

She gave him a cloak.

"With this you will be invisible and can
follow the princesses without being seen."
She said good-bye and went on her way.

The soldier went to the king
and was led to a room attached
to that of the princesses.
He did not drink the wine
that was brought to him,
and he pretended to snore.

When the princesses heard the soldier snore,
they laughed and quickly got up and got dressed.

Believing that the soldier was sound asleep,
the eldest princess went to her bed and tapped it.

Suddenly, it sank into the floor and the princesses ran down
a dark passageway. The soldier put on his cloak and followed.
The youngest princess thought she heard someone following them.
"Don't be silly. There is no one there," said the eldest.

Soon the princesses reached a grove of trees with silver leaves.
Then they came to one of gold leaves and one of diamond leaves.
The soldier broke off a twig from each.

They came to a lake where twelve princes were waiting in twelve boats. The invisible soldier sat in the boat with the youngest princess, and the prince wondered why it was so difficult to row.

They all reached the other side,
where there were lights and music.

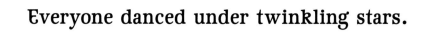

Everyone danced under twinkling stars.

The princesses danced on and on until their shoes were danced through and they could dance no longer.

The princes rowed them
back to shore, where they
all promised to meet
the next night.

The soldier ran ahead so the princesses found him
sound asleep when they returned.

He followed them the next two nights,
and on the last night he took a cup away with him.

The time arrived for
the soldier to speak
with the king.

"Where do my twelve
daughters go at night?"
the king asked.

"To a place underground
where they dance with
twelve princes,"
the soldier replied.

Then he told the king
what he had seen and
showed him the three
branches and the cup.

The king called for his daughters and
asked if the soldier spoke the truth.
Knowing that their secret had been
discovered, they confessed.

The soldier chose the eldest princess
for his wife, as he was not very young.
They were married that very day . . .

. . . and everyone danced and
danced all through the night.

For Gillian, the dancer

G. P. PUTNAM'S SONS

A division of Penguin Young Readers Group. Published by The Penguin Group. Penguin Group (USA) Inc., 375 Hudson Street, New York, NY 10014, U.S.A.

Penguin Group (Canada), 90 Eglinton Avenue East, Suite 700, Toronto, Ontario, Canada M4P 2Y3 (a division of Pearson Penguin Canada Inc.).

Penguin Books Ltd, 80 Strand, London WC2R 0RL, England. Penguin Ireland, 25 St. Stephen's Green, Dublin 2, Ireland (a division of Penguin Books Ltd.).

Penguin Group (Australia), 250 Camberwell Road, Camberwell, Victoria 3124, Australia (a division of Pearson Australia Group Pty Ltd).

Penguin Books India Pvt Ltd, 11 Community Centre, Panchsheel Park, New Delhi - 110 017, India.

Penguin Group (NZ), 67 Apollo Drive, Mairangi Bay, Auckland 1311, New Zealand (a division of Pearson New Zealand Ltd.).

Penguin Books (South Africa) (Pty) Ltd, 24 Sturdee Avenue, Rosebank, Johannesburg 2196, South Africa. Penguin Books Ltd, Registered Offices: 80 Strand, London WC2R 0RL, England.

Manufactured in China by South China Printing Co. Ltd. Design by Marikka Tamura. Text set in Geist. The illustrations were done with oil paints, printed paper and palette paper.
Library of Congress Cataloging-in-Publication Data
Isadora, Rachel. The twelve dancing princesses / [originally] written by the Brothers Grimm ; illustrated by Rachel Isadora. p. cm.
Summary: A retelling, set in Africa, of the story of twelve princesses who dance secretly all night long and how their secret is eventually discovered.
[1. Fairy tales. 2. Folklore—Germany.] I. Grimm, Jacob, 1785–1863. II. Grimm, Wilhelm, 1786–1859. III. Zertanzten Schuhe. English. IV. Title.
PZ8.I84Tw 2007   398.2—dc22   [E]   2007008160   ISBN 978-0-399-24744-6
1 3 5 7 9 10 8 6 4 2
First Impression